D1178158

# The Puffin Problem

# The
# Puffin Problem

## by Lori Doody

for Christopher and for Claire

There once was a city by the sea
with a peculiar problem.

Puffins were popping up everywhere.

Nobody knew what they were doing there,
and nobody knew why they had come.

Maybe they were distracted by the bright city lights.

Maybe they were drawn

to the rows of brightly painted houses.

Maybe they were delighted

with all of the seafood restaurants.

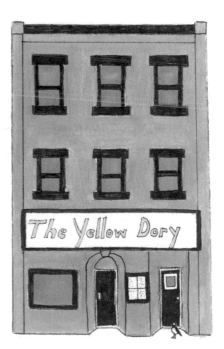

Whatever the reason,
they were showing up in unexpected places.

They were particularly prone
to visiting the downtown area,

and there were just too many of them.

They were tying up traffic.

They were bad for business.

They were overhead.

They were underfoot.

They were making
pets and pigeons uncomfortable.

Worst of all,
they were getting in the way
of everyone's fun.

A few birdwatchers were happy to see them,
but everyone else wanted them to leave.
People started gathering them up in hopes
of shipping them far, far away.

However, that idea didn't fly.
Eventually, someone small and smart came up
with a better plan to make the puffins go away.

The city folk agreed. Some seafood shops donated fish,

and a boat was loaded up to lead the puffins out to sea.

Luckily, the girl's idea worked,
and the peculiar visitors followed the boat
out of the harbour and off to the ocean.

The puffin problem was solved.

Well, at least until the next year…

In the summer, hundreds of thousands of Atlantic Puffins nest
on the rocky cliffs and islands south of St. John's, Newfoundland.
As summer ends, they fly out to sea where they spend most of the year.

Young puffins leaving their burrows use the stars and the moon
to navigate their way to the open ocean for the first time.
However, they can become disoriented by artificial lights in coastal
communities, and end up stranded on land. Kind volunteers join
the Puffin Patrol to help the young puffins find their way out to sea.
These people look for lost puffins at night and release them the next day.

While St. John's has never had an influx of puffins, it is fun to imagine
them visiting the downtown area.

On page 16, a puffin visits The Rooms Provincial Art Gallery and admires
Anne Meredith Barry's "Whale Song #10" (acrylic on canvas, 1989).
The painting is represented here with the kind permission of the Estate
of Anne Meredith Barry. Thanks to John Barry for his support of,
and enthusiasm for, this project.

# SOME FUN PUFFIN FACTS

The Atlantic Puffin is the official bird of Newfoundland and Labrador.

A group of puffins can be called a circus, a parliament, or an improbability.

A baby puffin can be called a puffling.

Around half of the world's Atlantic puffin population nests on the coastlines of Iceland.

In the wintertime, the puffins' colourful beaks turn grey.

Lori Doody was born in St. John's, Newfoundland,
and studied printmaking at Sir Wilfred Grenfell College;
she graduated in 1998. In 2005 she was named Emerging Artist of the Year
by the Newfoundland and Labrador Arts Council.
She lives in St. John's with her husband, their two children and their dog.
She likes puffins, but prefers them in their proper place.
*The Puffin Problem* is her second picture book.
You can see more of Lori's artwork at: www.loridoody.com

Text and illustrations ©2017 by Lori Doody

All rights reserved. No part of this publication may be reproduced
in any form without the prior written consent of the publisher.

The typeface is Adobe Garamond.
This book was designed by Veselina Tomova
of Vis-à-Vis Graphics,
St. John's, Newfoundland and Labrador,
and printed by Friesens in Canada.

978-1-927917-14-5

Running the Goat
Books & Broadsides, Inc.
54 Cove Road
Tors Cove, Newfoundland and Labrador A0A 4A0
www.runningthegoat.com